This book was gifted to

_____

with love from

_____

For Jordan:
May you always
get to share this story

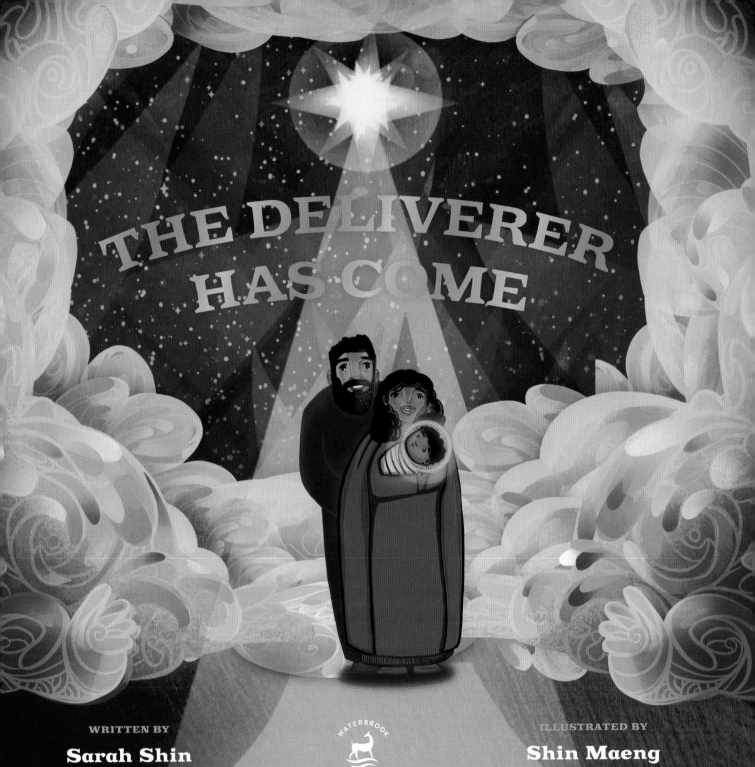

THE DELIVERER HAS COME

WRITTEN BY
Sarah Shin

WATERBROOK

ILLUSTRATED BY
Shin Maeng

Anika loved stories. And the stories she loved most
were the ones her great-auntie Anna told her.

Stories about a God who created a good and beautiful world.
And stories about their people, whom God chose to be His own.

In the past, their people trusted God, and they defeated giants, lions, and kings. But their people also often forgot to trust God and suffered through hard times, slavery, and exile. Yet God always promised to rescue them if they turned to Him again.

These stories gave Anika hope . . . because their people were waiting to be saved by the Deliverer whom God promised would end their suffering.

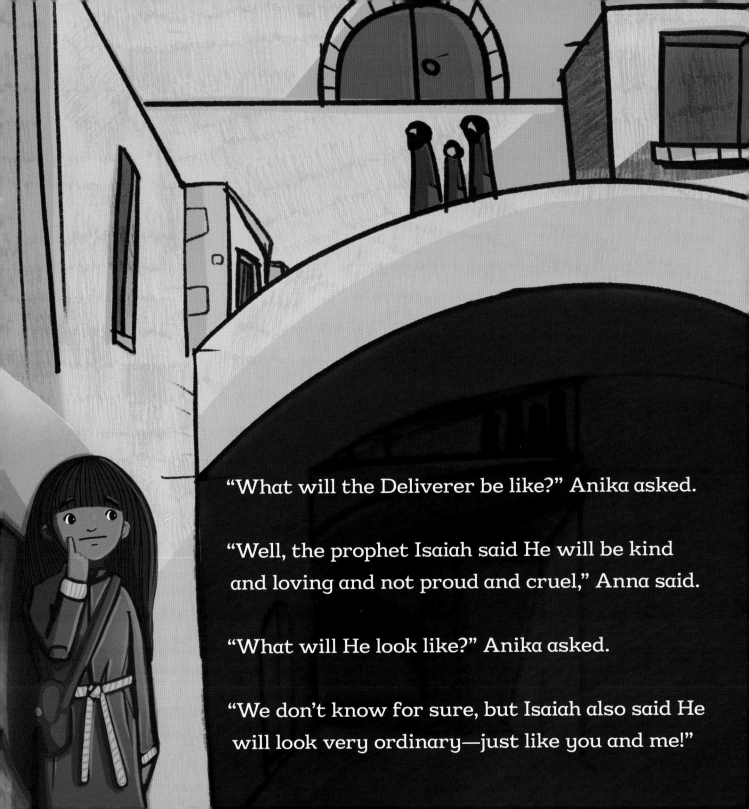

"What will the Deliverer be like?" Anika asked.

"Well, the prophet Isaiah said He will be kind and loving and not proud and cruel," Anna said.

"What will He look like?" Anika asked.

"We don't know for sure, but Isaiah also said He will look very ordinary—just like you and me!"

"How will He deliver us?" Anika asked.

"He will be filled with God's own Spirit," Anna answered. "He will come to set us free and heal our broken hearts. He will be good and show us how to love Him and how to love one another."

Anika sighed. *When will the Deliverer come?*

One night, Anika woke up to the most beautiful sound of singing. Glowing angels filled the sky!

"The Deliverer has come! Emmanuel God has come to His people tonight!"

"The Deliverer?" Anika gasped.

She listened until the angels and their song faded into the night.

Then a group of shepherds passed by.

"The Deliverer we have been waiting for has come!" they cried.
"The angels sang in the sky and told us how to find Him."

"Where? Where is the Deliverer?" Anika called after them.

Bethlehem? In a manger," one replied.

I wish I could see the Deliverer, Anika thought
as the shepherd continued on his way.

Over a month later, when Anika visited her great-aunt,
Anna was glowing with happiness.

"The Deliverer was here! His family brought Him to the temple, and I got to hold Him! I spoke to the people there about God's promise to redeem us," Anna proclaimed. "He's just a tiny baby, but seeing His face filled my heart with deep hope."

Anika was both happy and sad.
She was happy that Great-auntie
Anna got to see the Deliverer.
But Anika was sad that *she* still
had not seen Him!

When will it be my turn? she wondered,
looking out into the stars.

One evening, Anika noticed a star that
twinkled and danced more than the others.
Each night, it grew brighter and brighter.

On the night it shone its brightest,
it seemed to say to her, "Come!"

The star lit her path and
led Anika to a small house.

As she approached it, a group of
important-looking men stepped out.
They spoke in hushed voices, but Anika
was close enough to hear their words.

"We have seen the One we traveled all this
way to behold! The promised King in Israel's
story, the Deliverer! Here, under this star."

Anika was unable to contain her excitement.

"Where?" she asked, surprising them all.

"I have been waiting to meet Him too!"

The men smiled at her and gently gestured toward the open door.

Could it be? Will I finally meet the Deliverer? she wondered.

Inside the house, Anika saw a man,
a woman, and a baby boy.

"Hello, little one," the woman said.
"Did you follow the star here,
just like the wise men?"

Anika nodded.

The woman smiled at her
and said, "Come and see."

"Is He the Deliverer?" Anika asked, looking at the cheerful child. "He's so small and human—just like me. How could He rescue us?"

"I do not understand it all, but I believe what the angel told me," the woman replied. "This little one will grow to be a great teacher, healer, and deliverer. He will save the world and deliver us from our sins. He is God with us. His name is Jesus."

"Can I hold Him, please?" Anika asked.

"Yes, go ahead," the woman said.

Anika carefully picked up the child. She looked into
His eyes and felt a warm, cozy feeling.

"We've been waiting for You," she whispered. "I feel like
the whole world has been waiting for You to come."

And then she prayed . . .

Thank You, God, that I can tell this story of meeting the Deliverer, whose name is Jesus. May He grow strong and loving and save our broken and hurting world. May He make the greatest stories come to life.

The Story of Creation
Genesis 1–2

Noah's Ark
Genesis 6:9–9:17

A GUIDE TO
Anna and Anika's Stories

If you are interested in learning more about the stories shown through the illustrations in *The Deliverer Has Come*, the Scripture references are provided here.

God's Promise to Abraham
Genesis 12:1-9; Genesis 15:1-6

Moses and the Burning Bush
Exodus 3:1-12

**A Psalm About God as
Our Refuge**
Psalm 91:1-6

**The Deliverance of
Israel from Egypt**
Exodus 13:17–14:31

The Battle of Jericho
Joshua 5:13–6:27

David and Goliath
1 Samuel 17

**Shadrach, Meshach,
and Abednego**
Daniel 3

Daniel and the Lions' Den
Daniel 6

The Story of Jonah
Jonah 1–4

**God's Promise of Comfort
for Judah in Exile**
2 Kings 24–25; Isaiah 40:1–11

The Birth of Jesus
Luke 2:1–21

Anna Meets Baby Jesus
Luke 2:22–38

**The Wise Men Visit
Jesus**
Matthew 2:1–12

Published in the United States by WaterBrook,
an imprint of Random House, a division of
Penguin Random House LLC.

WATERBROOK and colophon are registered trademarks of
Penguin Random House LLC.

ISBN 978-0-593-58058-5
Ebook ISBN 978-0-593-58059-2

The Library of Congress catalog record is
available at https://lccn.loc.gov/2023002301.

Printed in China

waterbrookmultnomah.com

9 8 7 6 5 4 3 2 1

First Edition

Book and cover design by Ashley Tucker

Most WaterBrook books are available at special quantity
discounts for bulk purchase for premiums, fundraising,
and corporate and educational needs by organizations,
churches, and businesses. Special books or book excerpts
also can be created to fit specific needs. For details, contact
specialmarketscms@penguinrandomhouse.com.